Love me or hate me

Bris
grandma

Angel
Jonathan
grandpa
Galaxy
Titan
me Jesus

Daddy grandman Nancy Tia CHikis

nobody
Yay!!!

icecrem is better
icecrem is better
ice crem is better
up here and pard a is bad here
down here

Love me
pepple
Ti Gera dad beer Love me
twyla max

Love me
Ti o cone

When you're not looking...

A STORYTIME COUNTING BOOK

MAGGIE KNEEN

Simon & Schuster Books for Young Readers

For James

— M. K.

What do you think happens when you're not looking? Perhaps when you leave the room or turn your back or close your eyes or daydream, all the toys in the toy box scatter to different corners to enjoy their own adventures. Perhaps when you're not looking marionettes dance, toy planes fly, and mice search the attic for a hidden treasure. . . . Why are the puppets dancing? Where are the toy planes going? What are the mice looking for?

Each picture in this book includes objects or characters for you to find, hidden in different, fanciful settings. Each picture also captures one moment in a story and those stories are waiting here for you to find them, too.

There are as many stories in this book as you can imagine. Look for them. Enjoy them.

—*Maggie Kneen*

*The only sounds were the crackling
of the fire and a muffled thump from the window seat.*

"That's funny," said the kitten. *"I just saw her a few minutes ago."*

OPEN

As soon as it was dark, the mischief began again.

4

There hadn't been an audience in years,
but the puppets hardly noticed. Only Amanda was unhappy.

The planes knew exactly what to do next.

"Have you looked near the window yet?" asked the Rocking Horse.

7

"It's true," he declared. "I'll show you."

8

"Someday I'll go, too," she thought as she watched the ship sail away.

It would be a long journey.

"It's time!" Annabelle called to her sisters.

SIMON & SCHUSTER BOOKS FOR YOUNG READERS
An imprint of Simon & Schuster Children's Publishing Division
1230 Avenue of the Americas, New York, New York 10020

SIMON & SCHUSTER BOOKS FOR YOUNG READERS is a trademark of Simon & Schuster.
Book design by Heather Wood
The text for this book is set in Stempel Garamond.
The illustrations are rendered in watercolor, gouache, and pencil.
Printed and bound in the United States of America
First Edition
1 3 5 7 9 10 8 6 4 2

Library of Congress Cataloging-in-Publication Data
Kneen, Maggie.
When you're not looking : a storytime counting book / Maggie Kneen.—1st ed.
p.   cm.
Summary: Readers are encouraged to make up their own stories
and to find objects from one to ten in a series of detailed, fanciful illustrations.
ISBN 0-689-80026-6 (hc)
[1. Picture puzzles. 2. Counting.] I. Title
PZ7.K7338Wf   1996   95-51073   [E]—dc20

I Love to ~~read~~ read!!!! treehouse

New
York
York